THE LIFE AND DEATH OF CARMELITA BASINGSTOKE

A SHORT STORY

ALEXANDRIA BLAELOCK

BlueMere Books
MELBOURNE, AUSTRALIA

Publisher's Note: This is a work of fiction. Names, characters, places, and incidents are a product of the author's imagination. Locations and public names are sometimes used for atmospheric purposes. Any resemblance to actual people, living or dead, or to businesses, companies, events, institutions, or locations is completely coincidental.

Copyright © 2020 Alexandria Blaelock.

All rights reserved. No part of this publication may be reproduced, distributed or transmitted in any form or by any means, including photocopying, recording, or other electronic or mechanical methods, without the prior written permission of the publisher, except in the case of brief quotations embodied in critical reviews and certain other non-commercial uses permitted by copyright law.

For permission requests, please contact enquiries@bluemerebooks.com.

Ordering Information:
Discounts are available on quantity purchases. For details, contact orders@bluemerebooks.com.

The Life and Death of Carmelita Basingstoke/Alexandria Blaelock
paperback ISBN: 978-1-925749-28-1
digital ISBN: 978-1-925749-29-8

Book Layout © BookDesignTemplates.com

THE LIFE AND DEATH OF CARMELITA BASINGSTOKE

Carmelita Basingstoke eased through the gap in the fence of the Pioneer Cemetery.

This did mean climbing through a thick patch of rampant blackberry immediately on the other side, but at least she didn't have to walk around the acre plot to reach the main entrance.

Not that there was any reason to avoid it, aside from a long hot walk in the full glare of the midsummer sun.

It was just that fighting the blackberry seemed the lesser of two evils.

And in any case, she'd followed this path so many times before, the blackberry had almost given up the fight.

She used her backpack as a shield against the rest.

It's not like the cemetery was crowded with visitors - the surviving Abbots, Bennetts and Elliots had long since moved away leaving it mostly deserted.

And it had been closed to new burials for over a century since St Michael's Presbyterian church burned down in mysterious circumstances.

The only people she was likely to meet were either dead or members of the local historical society doing some research or restoration.

Though that was usually just weekend working bees. Not lunchtime midweek.

All she really wanted was a little peace and quiet.

A break from the trying and emotional routine that was establishing itself.

There had been too much living recently, and she just wasn't used to that.

She took a seat on the scratchy parched buffalo grass under a gum tree, its limp leaves hanging listlessly.

It wasn't the best shade tree in the universe, but its leaves waved languidly in the slightest breath of air, and that somehow made you feel cooler.

Even though the breeze wasn't enough to evaporate the sweat from your face. Or maybe it was the fresh scent of its insect repelling oil haze.

She blotted her face and neck with one of her late father's handkerchiefs, ironically white with black borders, and sighed.

Crickets clicked half-heartedly nearby, and a flock of cockatoos bickered amiably above her.

It's weird how much living dying involves, especially when you're not the one who's dying.

All that talking - to doctors, carers, funeral directors, lawyers, bankers, insurers, utility providers, vets, real estate agents, auction houses.

All those times you had to control your emotions, impassively responding to overly effusive expressions of sympathy that went nowhere near offsetting the implacable bureaucracy.

All those times people tried to provoke you because you weren't displaying what they thought the appropriate amount of grief for someone who lost both parents within a week of each other.

It's a wonder she hadn't exploded into a vicious rage and maimed someone.

Like maybe the funeral director who'd threatened to cancel her mother's funeral four hours before it was due to take place.

She sighed again and opened her water bottle, taking a drink of the last of her mother's homemade orange cordial.

Well watered down of course; it was just as sickly sweet as she remembered, but somehow exactly the right kind of drink for the time.

With the possible exception of something alcoholic. And despite the temptation, she needed her faculties about her.

It had been a difficult morning spent sorting through her parents' possessions.

In some ways, it was quite convenient of them to die so close together, but it did mean twice the work, and twice the decisions.

And being an only child, she didn't have any siblings to share the load.

Not that she'd actually done much sorting, it was mostly reminiscing about objects, and not being able to let them go.

At this rate, it was going to take the rest of her life to clean out theirs.

And she didn't have the time, she had to fly back home for work in a week, so she really had to start making some progress.

She'd managed to pack two boxes of "keepers" to freight home, but maybe it would be easier to call the freight company back and have them come out and pack everything.

Despite the heat and her mental and physical exhaustion, she was too restless to sit for long.

She stood and walked along the cheerful dandelion infested path, examining the graves as she went.

She'd emigrated as a child, and grew up in a nuclear family that liked to keep itself to itself, so all those founding families sharing graves and neighbouring plots were incomprehensible.

She tried and failed to imagine what it must have been like to grow up in the middle of a community that consisted almost entirely of your relatives.

Up a slight rise, a lone headstone leaned drunkenly to one side, and she thought that would be her likely end.

Alone, perhaps with a good view.

Though she planned to be cremated and scattered, so there wouldn't be any kind of monument.

In the present circumstances, the stone seemed a bit melodramatic, so she decided to go take a look at it.

As she approached, she was trying to decide whether the burial was separate because the deceased was an outcast, or if it just happened to be the only interment in that area with a stone.

Without a map, it was impossible to know whether there were other graves nearby.

Not that it mattered, she wasn't actually interested, it was simply a puzzle to distract her tired and emotional mind.

The stone wasn't actually leaning; a chunk had broken off the top and was lying in pieces where it fell nearby.

It was old, weathered and stained with lichen making the short epitaph difficult to make out.

She took a step closer and pulled aside the tall wild grasses to read the stone, tracing the engraving with her finger.

Carmelita Basingstoke

Died 1917

And that was all.

A cloud obscured the sun, and the day suddenly grew silent.

All she could hear was buzzing in her ears as the blood drained to her feet.

She shook her head, rubbed her eyes and read it again.

Carmelita Basingstoke.

Who was this woman with her name who happened to turn up dead right here and now?

She looked around as if there would be a person or sign who could explain it to her, though obviously there wouldn't be.

Nothing would satisfy her now, but that she found out more.

She drained her cordial, shouldered her backpack and headed back to the house.

The house was a tiny old three-bedroom, one-bathroom weatherboard cottage in the middle of a large block.

Her parents had bought it almost fifty years before, shortly after their arrival in Australia.

When they discovered they were dying, they sold it to the nearby nursing home on condition they could live in it until they died.

The board of management intended to replace it with units. And the general lack of anything more than the most basic maintenance left it looking haunted and decrepit even before her parents had moved into hospice care.

And that was only days before her father died.

But the garden was still beautiful, and the fruit and vegetable crops were flourishing.

So, Carmelita harvested some salad vegetables to go with the leftover take-out chicken.

And decided devil be damned, she needed a cocktail.

Coming from good English stock, there was plenty of gin and tonic in the house, with fresh lime from the big tree in the garden.

She hesitated a moment, and then made it a double.

The dining table was still cluttered with Lord knows what, and Carmelita was tempted for a moment to sweep it off onto the floor for somewhere to work.

But even intrigued by this new puzzle she couldn't bring herself to be so disrespectful of her parents' things.

She took her lunch and laptop onto the back verandah instead, within sniffing distance of the blooming heritage roses.

Firing up the computer, she took a sip of gin, and a bite of salad while she waited for it to warm up.

Another sip and another bite while she waited for it to pair with her phone, so she could connect to the Internet.

Then, wiggling her fingers in preparation, she started typing searches.

Nothing aside from herself under Carmelita Basingstoke on the first four pages, then variants of Carmen, Carmel, Carmella, Carmania, Carmelie, Carmesha, blah, blah, blah. More variations on the Basing theme - thwaite, ton, stone and so on.

Nothing!

That was annoying, but it was an unusual name. So unfortunate that the first one she met should be a century dead.

Mind you, if she'd been part of the Anne Smith club (three currently living in the same town) this wouldn't have been an issue.

Though how she'd know she had the right Anne Smith was another question. Assuming she'd care in the first place.

Though, come to think of it, how did she come to take up so much Internet space?

She ate a little more and took a big swig of her drink as she thought about what should be next.

Then she typed in the name of the cemetery, followed a few links here and there, and found the register of burials.

Which held no further information about Carmelita, and listed no further Basingstokes.

Though it did map the plot location as the Presbyterian section.

If she was in the Presbyterian section, a service had probably been held in the church.

Though it seemed likely the church records were lost in the fire so, they weren't going to be much help.

Another search revealed the historical society was open Monday and Thursday afternoons, and today was Tuesday. She wrote a quick email.

> "I noticed the grave of Carmelita Basingstoke in the Pioneer Cemetery, and as we share a name, I am intrigued.
>
> "I haven't found anything about her on the net, can you tell me more?"

Carmelita finished her lunch while she thought about how she might progress her research, but nothing sprang to mind.

She wondered, for a moment, why she was bothering about the late Carmelita Basingstoke.

Was it just that they shared the name?

Whatever the reason, going by what she'd paid for her parents' headstones, someone loved the late Carmelita Basingstoke enough to shell out a large fortune to ensure she wasn't forgotten.

Temporarily stalled on the late Carmelita Basingstoke front, it was time to get on with the reason she was here; disposing of her parents' belongings.

She shut down her phone and laptop, cleared up the dishes and prepared to return to the house.

But the plastic fly repelling ribbons hanging in the open back door suddenly felt like a mystic gateway to a place where time stood still, and the thought of entering the quiet, lifeless house was almost too much.

Though what the alternative was, she had no idea. She closed her eyes, took a deep breath and pushed through.

After dropping her things on the previously sacrosanct dining table, she walked from room to room opening all the curtains and windows as far as they would go and turning on the ceiling fans to maximum.

Then she turned on the radio and found a station playing modern music, and turned the volume up.

That was much better.

Suddenly filled with energy, she decided to tackle the "easy" stuff.

She folded and taped another couple of boxes ready to pack, grabbed a big heavy-duty garbage bag from the roll and entered the bathroom.

Given the speed of their decline and death, it was almost as if they had just stepped out of the house for a moment.

Toothbrushes still in place, bin full of cotton pads and a congealed squirt of liquid soap still on the basin.

Definitely time to get sorting.

First, she grabbed all the towelling, took it to the laundry and put a quick wash on.

All the unopened packs went into a box for charity. All the opened packs she wasn't using, and the contents of the bin went in the bag.

She took the blade from her father's safety razor and wrapped the pieces in toilet paper. The razor went in her keep box and the blade in the bag.

After a moment's thought, she retrieved their colognes from the garbage and wrapped them for her keep box as well.

She took the rubbish out, gave the room a cursory clean and hung the towels on the line to dry. That was it - first room down!

She'd been dreading doing their bedroom, but decided to tackle that next.

Carmelita was stunned by the strength of their scent in the room, even with the window wide open.

She staggered to the bed and flopped down on it, taking several deep breaths through her nose to try and imprint their smell deep in her memory.

Memories threatened to overwhelm her; sheltering under their covers from thunderstorms, enjoying morning cups of tea, watching her mother apply makeup.

Things that would never happen again, because they were gone, and the only place she would see them would be her dreams.

Her eyes flooded with tears, and she rolled herself in the blankets and allowed herself to cry for a time.

But she was mostly a practical woman, and there was too much to do to waste too much time.

She blew her nose on another of her father's hankies, then returned to the bathroom to wash her face and drink some water from the tap.

The woman in the mirror seemed a stranger; a tired, pale woman with dark circles under her eyes. Way past time she washed her hair.

She had her Dad's straight nose and dark eyes, neatly positioned in the middle of her Mum's square face.

Dad's sense of humour peeked out from her laughter lines, and Mum's determination in the frown lines between her eyes.

Maybe now that she'd found them, she'd see them again every time she looked in the mirror.

Sheets in the wash, blankets and pillows on the line to air out.

She started pulling her father's clothes out of his wardrobe, folding the serviceable ones into the charity box, and throwing the stained and torn ones into a succession of garbage bags.

She was momentarily halted by the blue jumper with holes in the elbows, the one older than her that he wore for gardening in cooler weather.

Tears threatened again, and she buried her face in its worn softness.

It still smelled like him, so she tenderly folded it, put it into her keep box and gently patted it down.

Then turned back to his wardrobe and finished going through his clothes and shoes.

And that was beginning to feel like enough for the moment, so she hung the washing out, then surveyed the bags of rubbish and clothes for charity.

It was clear that the rubbish wouldn't fit in the bin, and if she left the charity stuff lying about it would get in her way.

She needed a skip for the rubbish, and to drop the charity stuff off somewhere.

First things first, a cup of tea.

Then back online to order a skip for the next day, and find the charity shop drop off hours.

She had half an hour to spare before it shut, so she left her tea cooling on the cluttered table, threw the stuff in the car, and took off to drop it off.

The charity store was near a Chinese restaurant, so she ordered a couple of dishes to go.

While she waited, she thought more about the late Carmelita Basingstoke.

Was she born here, or did she emigrate from the United Kingdom?

Say she was fifty when she died, then it was unlikely she was a convict, though she could have been the child of a convict. Or a gold miner.

Did she die locally, or was she away nursing during the First World War?

And what about her life? A lot had happened during that time.

Did she know about Ned Kelly the bushranger?

Did she read *The Man from Snowy River*?

Had she heard the song *Waltzing Matilda*?

She took her dinner back to the house and ate it from the containers in front of the TV news.

It appeared that a noted Prime Minister had died during the night, and the show was half obituary.

Which gave her an idea.

Grabbing the laptop and linking to her phone again, she opened up the National Library site and searched the newspaper archive for Carmelita Basingstoke.

And there she was, Friday, August 3, 1917.

> *"Information was received last Monday that the woman found by Ned Bennett washed up on the bank of the Peel River, has died suddenly of pneumonia.*
>
> *It is believed the young woman, who gave her name as Carmelita Basingstoke, was washed downriver during the severe thunderstorms in May.*
>
> *Miss Basingstoke was kindly nursed during this time by the Bennett family.*
>
> *Unfortunately, no relatives have been found.*
>
> *The remains were on Wednesday interred in the Kew Cemetery, and the funeral was well attended.*
>
> *The Bennetts have opened a subscription to erect a headstone, so Miss Basingstoke's family (should they be located) have somewhere to mourn.*

> *The Reverend Alex McKay conducted the service at the grave, and Messrs Johansen and Son were the undertakers."*

One small entry that raised more questions than it answered.

Compared with her own four pages on the Internet, the late Carmelita Basingstoke left very little evidence of her life.

She was essentially flotsam, washed up on the edges of Ned Bennett's life.

She'd moved one of the founding families sufficiently to not only care for her but to take up a subscription on her behalf as well.

So, maybe she'd made a larger impact than had been recorded.

It would be nice to think that this Ned, whoever he was, had fallen for her.

That perhaps their hope for a long and happy future together had been tragically taken from them.

Outside, as the red sun slowly set the horizon on fire, a flock of kookaburras started their evening laugh.

THE END

ABOUT THE AUTHOR

Alexandria Blaelock writes stories, some of them for *Ellery Queen's Mystery Magazine* and *Pulphouse Fiction Magazine*. She's also written four self-help books applying business techniques to personal matters like getting dressed, cleaning house, and feeding your friends.

As a recovering Project Manager, she's probably too fond of sticking to plan. She lives in a forest because she enjoys birdsong, the scent of gum leaves and the sun on her face. When not telecommuting to parallel universes from her Melbourne based imagination, she watches K-dramas, talks to animals, and drinks Campari. At the same time.

Discover more at www.alexandriablaelock.com.

OTHER SHORT STORIES BY ALEXANDRIA BLAELOCK

Kiss of Death
Long Weekend in the Snow
Shining Star
Phoenix Child
Ship in a Bottle
Lady of the Looking Glass
Simone Says Hands in the Air
Life in the Security Directorate
Fate in Your Hands
Love in the Security Directorate
Alma's Grace
Payton's Run
The Guardian's Vigil
The Life and Death of Carmelita Basingstoke
Balancing the Book

BOOKS BY ALEXANDRIA BLAELOCK

Stress Free Dinner Parties
Build Your Signature Wardrobe
Holistic Personal Finance
Ms Blaelock's Book of Minimally Viable Housekeeping

Lightning Source UK Ltd.
Milton Keynes UK
UKHW021023210820
368606UK00016B/1106